Silas and Elanor,
you are love's song—S.M.T.

for Jackson—K.A.M.

Heart Art
PUBLISHING

GOOD NIGHT, CHILD OF MINE
by Susanna Thornhill, illustrations by Kathryn Ann Myers
Published by Heart Art Publishing

Hardback ISBN: 979-8-9859993-0-3
Paperback ISBN: 979-8-9859993-1-0
Text & illustrations copyright 2021 by Heart Art Publishing
Cover and book design by Stella Mongodi

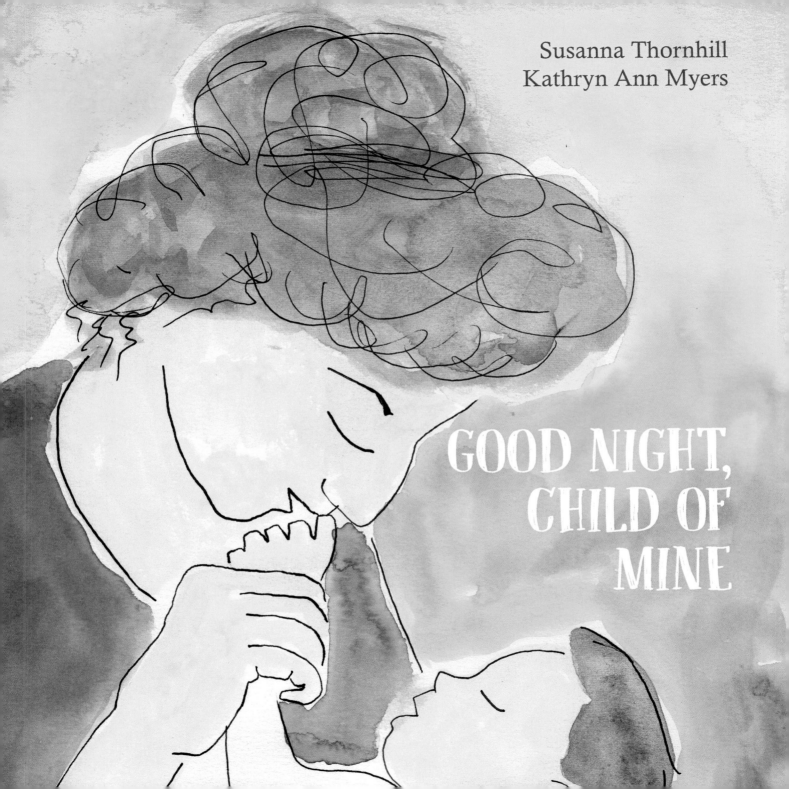

Susanna Thornhill
Kathryn Ann Myers

GOOD NIGHT,
CHILD OF
MINE

In a young child's room
stands cradle and chair;
a Mama softly breathes,
small hand in her hair.

Holding babe close,
as stars wheel above,
snuggling together,
she sings of the love.

This love is what ties,
the ties that bind tight,
like the rocker she sits in,
sturdy, soft, and white.

Love's song
floats by books,
lost socks,
and stuffed toys...

...it caresses the air
with its warm, sweet noise.

Love weaves its way through,
dissolving all fear.
It bathes us in light;
sweet dreams are so near.

Love holds tomorrow,
stands guard while we sleep.
It waits to sustain us
when shadows are deep.

Now lay your head down,
there's no need to fear,
Love's song is around you;
calm, sweet, and clear.

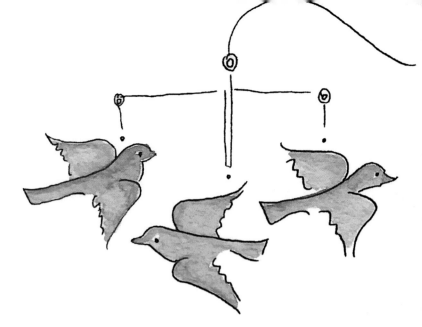

Wind up the mobile,
now hear it chime.
Good night and sleep tight...

...LITTLE CHILD OF MINE.

Made in the USA
Columbia, SC
15 March 2023

13839736R00015